Note To The Reader

This book is about a special relationship and grieving for a loved one who dies. I wrote this book for my niece many years ago when my father, her papa or grandpa, passed away. The book does not answer any questions but rather raises some. It explores feelings and emotions that a young child may experience during this time. My purpose in writing this book was to give comfort and support to young children and their families. Death is often a very difficult subject to approach. This book will provide you and your child with a tool for discussion. There is no age limit for this book, but it was intentionally written with language, vocabulary and style suitable for young children.

Judy Laufer

"I commend your ingenuity and creativity and certainly would highly recommend that this book be read by elementary school children and parents. You captured the reality and the uncertainty of the unknown."

Dr. Jeffrey L. Derevensky
Associate Professor and Director of Clinical Training
Dept. of Educational Psychology and Counselling
Associate Professor, Dept. of Psychiatry
McGill University, Montreal, Canada

"It is a sensitively written story about a topic which typically is very difficult to discuss with children. I know that the reaction to your book will be favorable when it is published. I know many teachers who would appreciate having access to it."

Dr. Paul H. Koehler
Associate Superintendent for Educational Services
Arizona Department of Education

Published by
LITTLE EGG®
PUBLISHING COMPANY
PHOENIX, ARIZONA

Especially for

. . .my wonderful mom, my tech-savvy brother, and sister
. . .Hayley, Jonathan and Darren–who inspired this book.
. . .Nathan, your support and encouragement.
. . .Andrew, named after his "Papa".
. . .all our family and friends, who loved him too.

Publisher's Cataloging-In-Publication Data
(Prepared by The Donohue Group, Inc.)

Laufer, Judy Egett.
   Where did papa go? / created and written by Judy Egett Laufer ;
illustrations by Ken S. Wingfield, Jr.

   p. : col. ill. ; cm.

   Reprint: 1990 ed., with minor changes.
   Summary: A young girl's simplistically touching poetic musing on the death of
her grandfather, who she affectionately calls "Papa."
   ISBN-13: 978-1-881669-00-5
   ISBN-10: 1-881669-00-9

   1. Grandfathers—Death—Juvenile fiction. 2. Grandparent and child-
-Juvenile fiction. 3. Grandfathers—Fiction. 4. Death—Fiction. 5. Stories in
rhyme. I. Wingfield, Ken S. II. Title.

PZ8.3.L346 Wh 1990
[E]

1st printing, 1991
2nd printing, fall 2012   Printed in the U.S.A.

Published by
LITTLE EGG
PUBLISHING COMPANY
PHOENIX, ARIZONA

WHERE DID PAPA GO?

Created and Written by Judy Egett Laufer
Illustrations by Ken S. Wingfield, Jr.

Papa's gone, why can't I see him anymore?

Why won't I see him when I walk through the door?

No more walks in the park.

Or listening together, to the neighbor's dog bark.   9

I know he loved me,
I hope he knew that I really loved him, a lot!

How much I've learned from him, how well he taught.

Is he visiting the sun or moon or stars?

I wonder if people up there drive cars?

**Can he see me,
does he know what I'm doing right now?**

I think he sees me, but I'm not sure how.

It's strange I can't see him, but I feel him inside. 21

I want to yell, "Come out you don't need to hide!"

I look and look but I can't see him,
No, not with my eyes.

And I guess that's what happens, when somebody dies.

We've shared so much, such special times,

I have such wonderful memories of him and I.

That for me, Papa will never really die!

In Memory of Papa

Though you are gone from these parts,
You will never be forgotten in our hearts!

About the Author

Judy Egett Laufer has been in the field of early childhood education for over 25 years. As a certified teacher and educational consultant, her primary interest was developing social and emotional skills in her young students. Judy worked in private and public schools in Canada and in the United States.

She was awarded the Golden Poet Award for this book, WHERE DID PAPA GO? in 1991. It was written as a tribute to her Dad, "Papa" to the grandchildren.

Judy is married and lives with her husband, Nathan and son, Andrew in the Southwest.